THE HISTORY OF DON QUIXOTE, VOLUME 1, PART 01
BY
Cervantes

THE HISTORY OF DON QUIXOTE, VOLUME 1, PART 01

Published by Silver Scroll Publishing

New York City, NY

First published circa 1616

ABOUT SILVER SCROLL PUBLISHING

Silver Scroll Publishing is a digital publisher that brings the best historical fiction ever written to modern readers. Our comprehensive catalogue contains everything from historical novels about Rome to works about World War I.

DON QUIXOTE: by Miguel de Cervantes: Translated by John Ormsby: Volume I., Part 1. Chapters 1-3

spine.jpg (152K)

TRANSLATOR'S PREFACE: I: ABOUT THIS TRANSLATION

It was with considerable reluctance that I abandoned in favour of the present undertaking what had long been a favourite project: that of a new edition of Shelton's "Don Quixote," which has now become a somewhat scarce book. There are some—and I confess myself to be one—for whom Shelton's racy old version, with all its defects, has a charm that no modern translation, however skilful or correct, could possess. Shelton had the inestimable advantage of belonging to the same generation as Cervantes; "Don Quixote" had to him a vitality that only a contemporary could feel; it cost him no dramatic effort to see things as Cervantes saw them; there is no anachronism in his language; he put the Spanish of Cervantes into the English of Shakespeare. Shakespeare himself most likely knew the book; he may have carried it home with him in his saddle-bags to Stratford on one of his last journeys, and under the mulberry tree at New Place joined hands with a kindred genius in its pages.

But it was soon made plain to me that to hope for even a moderate popularity for Shelton was vain. His fine old crusted English would, no doubt, be relished by a minority, but it would be only by a minority. His warmest admirers must admit that he is not a satisfactory representative of Cervantes. His translation of the First Part was very hastily made and was never revised by him. It has all the freshness and vigour, but also a full measure of the faults, of a hasty production. It is often very literal—barbarously literal frequently—but just as often very loose. He had evidently a good colloquial knowledge of Spanish, but apparently not much more. It never seems to occur to him that the same translation of a word will not suit in every case.

It is often said that we have no satisfactory translation of "Don Quixote." To those who are familiar with the original, it savours of truism or platitude to say so, for in truth there can be no thoroughly satisfactory translation of "Don Quixote" into English or any other language. It is not that the Spanish idioms are so utterly unmanageable, or that the untranslatable words, numerous enough no doubt, are so superabundant, but rather that the sententious terseness to which the humour of the book owes its flavour is peculiar to Spanish, and can at best be only distantly imitated in any other tongue.

The history of our English translations of "Don Quixote" is instructive. Shelton's, the first in any language, was made, apparently, about 1608, but not published till 1612. This of course was only the First Part. It has been asserted that the Second, published in 1620, is not the work of Shelton, but there is nothing to support the assertion save the fact that it has less spirit, less of what we generally understand by "go," about it than the first, which would be only natural if the first were the work of a young man writing currente calamo, and the second that of a middle-aged man writing for a bookseller. On the other hand, it is closer and more literal, the style is the same, the very same translations, or mistranslations, occur in it, and it is extremely unlikely that a new translator would, by suppressing his name, have allowed Shelton to carry off the credit.

In 1687 John Phillips, Milton's nephew, produced a "Don Quixote" "made English," he says, "according to the humour of our modern language." His "Quixote" is not so much a translation as a travesty, and a travesty that for coarseness, vulgarity, and buffoonery is almost unexampled even in the literature of that day.

Ned Ward's "Life and Notable Adventures of Don Quixote, merrily translated into Hudibrastic Verse" (1700), can scarcely be reckoned a translation, but it serves to show the light in which "Don Quixote" was regarded at the time.

A further illustration may be found in the version published in 1712 by Peter Motteux, who had then recently combined tea-dealing with literature. It is described as "translated from the original by several hands," but if so all Spanish flavour has entirely evaporated under the manipulation of the several hands. The flavour that it has, on the other hand, is distinctly Franco-cockney. Anyone who compares it carefully with the original will have little doubt that it is a concoction from Shelton and the French of Filleau de Saint Martin, eked out by borrowings from Phillips, whose mode of treatment it adopts. It is, to be sure, more decent and decorous, but it treats "Don Quixote" in the same fashion as a comic book that cannot be made too comic.

To attempt to improve the humour of "Don Quixote" by an infusion of cockney flippancy and facetiousness, as Motteux's operators did, is not merely an impertinence like larding a sirloin of prize beef, but an absolute falsification of the spirit of the book, and it is a proof of the uncritical way in which "Don Quixote" is generally read that this worse than worthless translation— worthless as failing to represent, worse than worthless as misrepresenting—should have been favoured as it has been.

It had the effect, however, of bringing out a translation undertaken and executed in a very different spirit, that of Charles Jervas, the portrait painter, and friend of Pope, Swift, Arbuthnot, and Gay. Jervas been allowed little credit for his work, indeed it may be said none, for it is known to the world in general as Jarvis's. It was not published until after his death, and the printers gave the name according to the current pronunciation of the day. It has been the most freely used and the most freely abused of all the translations. It has seen far more editions than any other, it is admitted on all hands to be by far the most faithful, and yet nobody seems to have a good word to say for it or for its author. Jervas no doubt prejudiced readers against himself in his preface, where among many true words about Shelton, Stevens, and Motteux, he rashly and unjustly charges Shelton with having translated not from the Spanish, but from the Italian version of Franciosini, which did not appear until ten years after Shelton's first volume. A suspicion of incompetence, too, seems to have attached to him because he was by profession a painter and a mediocre one (though he has given us the best portrait we have of Swift), and this may have been strengthened by Pope's remark that he "translated 'Don Quixote' without understanding Spanish." He has been also charged with borrowing from Shelton, whom he disparaged. It is true that in a few difficult or obscure passages he has followed Shelton, and gone astray with him; but for one case of this sort, there are fifty where he is right and Shelton wrong. As for Pope's dictum, anyone who examines Jervas's version carefully, side by side with the original, will see that he was a sound Spanish scholar, incomparably a better one than Shelton, except perhaps in mere colloquial Spanish. He was, in fact, an honest, faithful, and painstaking translator, and he has left a version which, whatever its shortcomings may be, is singularly free from errors and mistranslations.

The charge against it is that it is stiff, dry—"wooden" in a word,—and no one can deny that there is a foundation for it. But it may be pleaded for Jervas that a good deal of this rigidity is due to his abhorrence of the light, flippant, jocose style of his predecessors. He was one of the few, very few, translators that have shown any apprehension of the unsmiling gravity which is the essence of Quixotic humour; it seemed to him a crime to bring Cervantes forward smirking and grinning at his own good things, and to this may be attributed in a great measure the ascetic abstinence from everything savouring of liveliness which is the characteristic of his translation. In most modern editions, it should be observed, his style has been smoothed and smartened, but without any reference to the original Spanish, so that if he has been made to read more agreeably he has also been robbed of his chief merit of fidelity.

Smollett's version, published in 1755, may be almost counted as one of these. At any rate it is plain that in its construction Jervas's translation was very freely drawn upon, and very little or probably no heed given to the original Spanish.

The later translations may be dismissed in a few words. George Kelly's, which appeared in 1769, "printed for the Translator," was an impudent imposture, being nothing more than Motteux's version with a few of the words, here and there, artfully transposed; Charles Wilmot's (1774) was only an abridgment like Florian's, but not so skilfully executed; and the version published by Miss Smirke in 1818, to accompany her brother's plates, was merely a patchwork production made out of former translations. On the latest, Mr. A. J. Duffield's, it would be in every sense of the word impertinent in me to offer an opinion here. I had not even seen it when the present undertaking was proposed to me, and since then I may say vidi tantum, having for obvious reasons resisted the temptation which Mr. Duffield's reputation and comely volumes hold out to every lover of Cervantes.

From the foregoing history of our translations of "Don Quixote," it will be seen that there are a good many people who, provided they get the mere narrative with its full complement of facts, incidents, and adventures served up to them in a form that amuses them, care very little whether that form is the one in which Cervantes originally shaped his ideas. On the other hand, it is clear that there are many who desire to have not merely the story he tells, but the story as he tells it, so far at least as differences of idiom and circumstances permit, and who will give a preference to the conscientious translator, even though he may have acquitted himself somewhat awkwardly.

But after all there is no real antagonism between the two classes; there is no reason why what pleases the one should not please the other, or why a translator who makes it his aim to treat "Don Quixote" with the respect due to a great classic, should not be as acceptable even to the careless reader as the one who treats it as a famous old jest-book. It is not a question of caviare to the general, or, if it is, the fault rests with him who makes so. The method by which Cervantes won the ear of the Spanish people ought, mutatis mutandis, to be equally effective with the great majority of English readers. At any rate, even if there are readers to whom it is a matter of indifference, fidelity to the method is as much a part of the translator's duty as fidelity to the matter. If he can please all parties, so much the better; but his first duty is to those who look to him for as faithful a representation of his author as it is in his power to give them, faithful to the letter so long as fidelity is practicable, faithful to the spirit so far as he can make it.

My purpose here is not to dogmatise on the rules of translation, but to indicate those I have followed, or at least tried to the best of my ability to follow, in the present instance. One which, it seems to me, cannot be too rigidly followed in translating "Don Quixote," is to avoid everything that savours of affectation. The book itself is, indeed, in one sense a protest against it, and no man abhorred it more than Cervantes. For this reason, I think, any temptation to use antiquated or obsolete language should be resisted. It is after all an affectation, and one for which there is no warrant or excuse. Spanish has probably undergone less change since the seventeenth century than any language in Europe, and by far the greater and certainly the best part of "Don Quixote" differs but little in language from the colloquial Spanish of the present day. Except in the tales and Don Quixote's speeches, the translator who uses the simplest and plainest everyday language will almost always be the one who approaches nearest to the original.

Seeing that the story of "Don Quixote" and all its characters and incidents have now been for more than two centuries and a half familiar as household words in English mouths, it seems to me that the old familiar names and phrases should not be changed without good reason. Of course a translator who holds that "Don Quixote" should receive the treatment a great classic deserves, will feel himself bound by the injunction laid upon the Morisco in Chap. IX not to omit or add anything.

II: ABOUT CERVANTES AND DON QUIXOTE

Four generations had laughed over "Don Quixote" before it occurred to anyone to ask, who and what manner of man was this Miguel de Cervantes Saavedra whose name is on the title-page; and it was too late for a satisfactory answer to the question when it was proposed to add a life of the author to the London edition published at Lord Carteret's instance in 1738. All traces of the personality of Cervantes had by that time disappeared. Any floating traditions that may once have existed, transmitted from men who had known him, had long since died out, and of other record there was none; for the sixteenth and seventeenth centuries were incurious as to "the men of the time," a reproach against which the nineteenth has, at any rate, secured itself, if it has produced no Shakespeare or Cervantes. All that Mayans y Siscar, to whom the task was entrusted, or any of those who followed him, Rios, Pellicer, or Navarrete, could do was to eke out the few allusions Cervantes makes to himself in his various prefaces with such pieces of documentary evidence bearing upon his life as they could find.

This, however, has been done by the last-named biographer to such good purpose that he has superseded all predecessors. Thoroughness is the chief characteristic of Navarrete's work. Besides sifting, testing, and methodising with rare patience and judgment what had been previously brought to light, he left, as the saying is, no stone unturned under which anything to illustrate his subject might possibly be found. Navarrete has done all that industry and acumen could do, and it is no fault of his if he has not given us what we want. What Hallam says of Shakespeare may be applied to the almost parallel case of Cervantes: "It is not the register of his baptism, or the draft of his will, or the orthography of his name that we seek; no letter of his writing, no record of his conversation, no character of him drawn ... by a contemporary has been produced."

It is only natural, therefore, that the biographers of Cervantes, forced to make brick without straw, should have recourse largely to conjecture, and that conjecture should in some instances come by degrees to take the place of established fact. All that I propose to do here is to separate what is matter of fact from what is matter of conjecture, and leave it to the reader's judgment to decide whether the data justify the inference or not.

The men whose names by common consent stand in the front rank of Spanish literature, Cervantes, Lope de Vega, Quevedo, Calderon, Garcilaso de la Vega, the Mendozas, Gongora, were all men of ancient families, and, curiously, all, except the last, of families that traced their origin to the same mountain district in the North of Spain. The family of Cervantes is commonly said to have been of Galician origin, and unquestionably it was in possession of lands in Galicia at a very early date; but I think the balance of the evidence tends to show that the "solar," the original site of the family, was at Cervatos in the north-west corner of Old Castile, close to the junction of Castile, Leon, and the Asturias. As it happens, there is a complete history of the Cervantes family from the tenth century down to the seventeenth extant under the title of "Illustrious Ancestry, Glorious Deeds, and Noble Posterity of the Famous Nuno Alfonso, Alcaide of Toledo," written in 1648 by the industrious genealogist Rodrigo Mendez Silva, who availed himself of a manuscript genealogy by Juan de Mena, the poet laureate and historiographer of John II.

The origin of the name Cervantes is curious. Nuno Alfonso was almost as distinguished in the struggle against the Moors in the reign of Alfonso VII as the Cid had been half a century before in that of Alfonso VI, and was rewarded by divers grants of land in the neighbourhood of Toledo. On one of his acquisitions, about two leagues from the city, he built himself a castle which he called Cervatos, because "he was lord of the solar of Cervatos in the Montana," as the mountain region extending from the Basque Provinces to Leon was always called. At his death in battle in 1143, the castle passed by his will to his son Alfonso Munio, who, as territorial or local surnames were then coming into vogue in place of the simple patronymic, took the additional name of Cervatos. His eldest son Pedro succeeded him in the possession of the castle, and followed his example in adopting the name, an assumption at which the younger son, Gonzalo, seems to have taken umbrage.

Everyone who has paid even a flying visit to Toledo will remember the ruined castle that crowns the hill above the spot where the bridge of Alcantara spans the gorge of the Tagus, and with its broken outline and crumbling walls makes such an admirable pendant to the square solid Alcazar towering over the city roofs on the opposite side. It was built, or as some say restored, by Alfonso VI shortly after his occupation of Toledo in 1085, and called by him San Servando after a Spanish martyr, a name subsequently modified into San Servan (in which form it appears in the "Poem of the Cid"), San Servantes, and San Cervantes: with regard to which last the "Handbook for Spain" warns its readers against the supposition that it has anything to do with the author of "Don Quixote." Ford, as all know who have taken him for a companion and counsellor on the roads of Spain, is seldom wrong in matters of literature or history. In this instance, however, he is in error. It has everything to do with the author of "Don Quixote," for it is in fact these old walls that have given to Spain the name she is proudest of to-day. Gonzalo, above mentioned, it may be readily conceived, did not relish the appropriation by his brother of a name to which he himself had an equal right, for though nominally taken from the castle, it was in reality derived from the ancient territorial possession of the family, and as a set-off, and to distinguish himself (diferenciarse) from his brother, he took as a surname the name of the castle on the bank of the Tagus, in the building of which, according to a family tradition, his great-grandfather had a share.

Both brothers founded families. The Cervantes branch had more tenacity; it sent offshoots in various directions, Andalusia, Estremadura, Galicia, and Portugal, and produced a goodly line of men distinguished in the service of Church and State. Gonzalo himself, and apparently a son of his, followed Ferdinand III in the great campaign of 1236-48 that gave Cordova and Seville to Christian Spain and penned up the Moors in the kingdom of Granada, and his descendants intermarried with some of the noblest families of the Peninsula and numbered among them soldiers, magistrates, and Church dignitaries, including at least two cardinal-archbishops.

Of the line that settled in Andalusia, Deigo de Cervantes, Commander of the Order of Santiago, married Juana Avellaneda, daughter of Juan Arias de Saavedra, and had several sons, of whom one was Gonzalo Gomez, Corregidor of Jerez and ancestor of the Mexican and Columbian branches of the family; and another, Juan, whose son Rodrigo married Dona Leonor de Cortinas, and by her had four children, Rodrigo, Andrea, Luisa, and Miguel, our author.

The pedigree of Cervantes is not without its bearing on "Don Quixote." A man who could look back upon an ancestry of genuine knights-errant extending from well-nigh the time of Pelayo to the siege of Granada was likely to have a strong feeling on the subject of the sham chivalry of the romances. It gives a point, too, to what he says in more than one place about families that have once been great and have tapered away until they have come to nothing, like a pyramid. It was the case of his own.

He was born at Alcala de Henares and baptised in the church of Santa Maria Mayor on the 9th of October, 1547. Of his boyhood and youth we know nothing, unless it be from the glimpse he gives us in the preface to his "Comedies" of himself as a boy looking on with delight while Lope de Rueda and his company set up their rude plank stage in the plaza and acted the rustic farces which he himself afterwards took as the model of his interludes. This first glimpse, however, is a significant one, for it shows the early development of that love of the drama which exercised such an influence on his life and seems to have grown stronger as he grew older, and of which this very preface, written only a few months before his death, is such a striking proof. He gives us to understand, too, that he was a great reader in his youth; but of this no assurance was needed, for the First Part of "Don Quixote" alone proves a vast amount of miscellaneous reading, romances of chivalry, ballads, popular poetry, chronicles, for which he had no time or opportunity except in the first twenty years of his life; and his misquotations and mistakes in matters of detail are always, it may be noticed, those of a man recalling the reading of his boyhood.

Other things besides the drama were in their infancy when Cervantes was a boy. The period of his boyhood was in every way a transition period for Spain. The old chivalrous Spain had passed away. The new Spain was the mightiest power the world had seen since the Roman Empire and it had not yet been called upon to pay the price of its greatness. By the policy of Ferdinand and Ximenez the sovereign had been made absolute, and the Church and Inquisition adroitly adjusted to keep him so. The nobles, who had always resisted absolutism as strenuously as they had fought the Moors, had been divested of all political power, a like fate had befallen the cities, the free constitutions of Castile and Aragon had been swept away, and the only function that remained to the Cortes was that of granting money at the King's dictation.

The transition extended to literature. Men who, like Garcilaso de la Vega and Diego Hurtado de Mendoza, followed the Italian wars, had brought back from Italy the products of the post-Renaissance literature, which took root and flourished and even threatened to extinguish the native growths. Damon and Thyrsis, Phyllis and Chloe had been fairly naturalised in Spain, together with all the devices of pastoral poetry for investing with an air of novelty the idea of a dispairing shepherd and inflexible shepherdess. As a set-off against this, the old historical and traditional ballads, and the true pastorals, the songs and ballads of peasant life, were being collected assiduously and printed in the cancioneros that succeeded one another with increasing rapidity. But the most notable consequence, perhaps, of the spread of printing was the flood of romances of chivalry that had continued to pour from the press ever since Garci Ordonez de Montalvo had resuscitated "Amadis of Gaul" at the beginning of the century.

For a youth fond of reading, solid or light, there could have been no better spot in Spain than Alcala de Henares in the middle of the sixteenth century. It was then a busy, populous university town, something more than the enterprising rival of Salamanca, and altogether a very different place from the melancholy, silent, deserted Alcala the traveller sees now as he goes from Madrid to Saragossa. Theology and medicine may have been the strong points of the university, but the town itself seems to have inclined rather to the humanities and light literature, and as a producer of books Alcala was already beginning to compete with the older presses of Toledo, Burgos, Salamanca and Seville.

A pendant to the picture Cervantes has given us of his first playgoings might, no doubt, have been often seen in the streets of Alcala at that time; a bright, eager, tawny-haired boy peering into a book-shop where the latest volumes lay open to tempt the public, wondering, it may be, what that little book with the woodcut of the blind beggar and his boy, that called itself "Vida de Lazarillo de Tormes, segunda impresion," could be about; or with eyes brimming over with merriment gazing at one of those preposterous portraits of a knight-errant in outrageous panoply and plumes with which the publishers of chivalry romances loved to embellish the title-pages of their folios. If the boy was the father of the man, the sense of the incongruous that was strong at fifty was lively at ten, and some such reflections as these may have been the true genesis of "Don Quixote."

For his more solid education, we are told, he went to Salamanca. But why Rodrigo de Cervantes, who was very poor, should have sent his son to a university a hundred and fifty miles away when he had one at his own door, would be a puzzle, if we had any reason for supposing that he did so. The only evidence is a vague statement by Professor Tomas Gonzalez, that he once saw an old entry of the matriculation of a Miguel de Cervantes. This does not appear to have been ever seen again; but even if it had, and if the date corresponded, it would prove nothing, as there were at least two other Miguels born about the middle of the century; one of them, moreover, a Cervantes Saavedra, a cousin, no doubt, who was a source of great embarrassment to the biographers.

That he was a student neither at Salamanca nor at Alcala is best proved by his own works. No man drew more largely upon experience than he did, and he has nowhere left a single reminiscence of student life—for the "Tia Fingida," if it be his, is not one—nothing, not even "a college joke," to show that he remembered days that most men remember best. All that we know positively about his education is that Juan Lopez de Hoyos, a professor of humanities and belles-lettres of some eminence, calls him his "dear and beloved pupil." This was in a little collection of verses by different hands on the death of Isabel de Valois, second queen of Philip II, published by the professor in 1569, to which Cervantes contributed four pieces, including an elegy, and an epitaph in the form of a sonnet. It is only by a rare chance that a "Lycidas" finds its way into a volume of this sort, and Cervantes was no Milton. His verses are no worse than such things usually are; so much, at least, may be said for them.

By the time the book appeared he had left Spain, and, as fate ordered it, for twelve years, the most eventful ones of his life. Giulio, afterwards Cardinal, Acquaviva had been sent at the end of 1568 to Philip II by the Pope on a mission, partly of condolence, partly political, and on his return to Rome, which was somewhat brusquely expedited by the King, he took Cervantes with him as his camarero (chamberlain), the office he himself held in the Pope's household. The post would no doubt have led to advancement at the Papal Court had Cervantes retained it, but in the summer of 1570 he resigned it and enlisted as a private soldier in Captain Diego Urbina's company, belonging to Don Miguel de Moncada's regiment, but at that time forming a part of the command of Marc Antony Colonna. What impelled him to this step we know not, whether it was distaste for the career before him, or purely military enthusiasm. It may well have been the latter, for it was a stirring time; the events, however, which led to the alliance between Spain, Venice, and the Pope, against the common enemy, the Porte, and to the victory of the combined fleets at Lepanto, belong rather to the history of Europe than to the life of Cervantes. He was one of those that sailed from Messina, in September 1571, under the command of Don John of Austria; but on the morning of the 7th of October, when the Turkish fleet was sighted, he was lying below ill with fever. At the news that the enemy was in sight he rose, and, in spite of the remonstrances of his comrades and superiors, insisted on taking his post, saying he preferred death in the service of God and the King to health. His galley, the Marquesa, was in the thick of the fight, and before it was over he had received three gunshot wounds, two in the breast and one in the left hand or arm. On the morning after the battle, according to Navarrete, he had an interview with the commander-in-chief, Don John, who was making a personal inspection of the wounded, one result of which was an addition of three crowns to his pay, and another, apparently, the friendship of his general.

How severely Cervantes was wounded may be inferred from the fact, that with youth, a vigorous frame, and as cheerful and buoyant a temperament as ever invalid had, he was seven months in hospital at Messina before he was discharged. He came out with his left hand permanently disabled; he had lost the use of it, as Mercury told him in the "Viaje del Parnaso" for the greater glory of the right. This, however, did not absolutely unfit him for service, and in April 1572 he joined Manuel Ponce de Leon's company of Lope de Figueroa's regiment, in which, it seems probable, his brother Rodrigo was serving, and shared in the operations of the next three years, including the capture of the Goletta and Tunis. Taking advantage of the lull which followed the recapture of these places by the Turks, he obtained leave to return to Spain, and sailed from Naples in September 1575 on board the Sun galley, in company with his brother Rodrigo, Pedro Carrillo de Quesada, late Governor of the Goletta, and some others, and furnished with letters from Don John of Austria and the Duke of Sesa, the Viceroy of Sicily, recommending him to the King for the command of a company, on account of his services; a dono infelice as events proved. On the 26th they fell in with a squadron of Algerine galleys, and after a stout resistance were overpowered and carried into Algiers.

By means of a ransomed fellow-captive the brothers contrived to inform their family of their condition, and the poor people at Alcala at once strove to raise the ransom money, the father disposing of all he possessed, and the two sisters giving up their marriage portions. But Dali Mami had found on Cervantes the letters addressed to the King by Don John and the Duke of Sesa, and, concluding that his prize must be a person of great consequence, when the money came he refused it scornfully as being altogether insufficient. The owner of Rodrigo, however, was more easily satisfied; ransom was accepted in his case, and it was arranged between the brothers that he should return to Spain and procure a vessel in which he was to come back to Algiers and take off Miguel and as many of their comrades as possible. This was not the first attempt to escape that Cervantes had made. Soon after the commencement of his captivity he induced several of his companions to join him in trying to reach Oran, then a Spanish post, on foot; but after the first day's journey, the Moor who had agreed to act as their guide deserted them, and they had no choice but to return. The second attempt was more disastrous. In a garden outside the city on the sea-shore, he constructed, with the help of the gardener, a Spaniard, a hiding-place, to which he brought, one by one, fourteen of his fellow-captives, keeping them there in secrecy for several months, and supplying them with food through a renegade known as El Dorador, "the Gilder." How he, a captive himself, contrived to do all this, is one of the mysteries of the story. Wild as the project may appear, it was very nearly successful. The vessel procured by Rodrigo made its appearance off the coast, and under cover of night was proceeding to take off the refugees, when the crew were alarmed by a passing fishing boat, and beat a hasty retreat. On renewing the attempt shortly afterwards, they, or a portion of them at least, were taken prisoners, and just as the poor fellows in the garden were exulting in the thought that in a few moments more freedom would be within their grasp, they found themselves surrounded by Turkish troops, horse and foot. The Dorador had revealed the whole scheme to the Dey Hassan.

When Cervantes saw what had befallen them, he charged his companions to lay all the blame upon him, and as they were being bound he declared aloud that the whole plot was of his contriving, and that nobody else had any share in it. Brought before the Dey, he said the same. He was threatened with impalement and with torture; and as cutting off ears and noses were playful freaks with the Algerines, it may be conceived what their tortures were like; but nothing could make him swerve from his original statement that he and he alone was responsible. The upshot was that the unhappy gardener was hanged by his master, and the prisoners taken possession of by the Dey, who, however, afterwards restored most of them to their masters, but kept Cervantes, paying Dali Mami 500 crowns for him. He felt, no doubt, that a man of such resource, energy, and daring, was too dangerous a piece of property to be left in private hands; and he had him heavily ironed and lodged in his own prison. If he thought that by these means he could break the spirit or shake the resolution of his prisoner, he was soon undeceived, for Cervantes contrived before long to despatch a letter to the Governor of Oran, entreating him to send him some one that could be trusted, to enable him and three other gentlemen, fellow-captives of his, to make their escape; intending evidently to renew his first attempt with a more trustworthy guide. Unfortunately the Moor who carried the letter was stopped just outside Oran, and the letter being found upon him, he was sent back to Algiers, where by the order of the Dey he was promptly impaled as a warning to others, while Cervantes was condemned to receive two thousand blows of the stick, a number which most likely would have deprived the world of "Don Quixote," had not some persons, who they were we know not, interceded on his behalf.

After this he seems to have been kept in still closer confinement than before, for nearly two years passed before he made another attempt. This time his plan was to purchase, by the aid of a Spanish renegade and two Valencian merchants resident in Algiers, an armed vessel in which he and about sixty of the leading captives were to make their escape; but just as they were about to put it into execution one Doctor Juan Blanco de Paz, an ecclesiastic and a compatriot, informed the Dey of the plot. Cervantes by force of character, by his self-devotion, by his untiring energy and his exertions to lighten the lot of his companions in misery, had endeared himself to all, and become the leading spirit in the captive colony, and, incredible as it may seem, jealousy of his influence and the esteem in which he was held, moved this man to compass his destruction by a cruel death. The merchants finding that the Dey knew all, and fearing that Cervantes under torture might make disclosures that would imperil their own lives, tried to persuade him to slip away on board a vessel that was on the point of sailing for Spain; but he told them they had nothing to fear, for no tortures would make him compromise anybody, and he went at once and gave himself up to the Dey.

As before, the Dey tried to force him to name his accomplices. Everything was made ready for his immediate execution; the halter was put round his neck and his hands tied behind him, but all that could be got from him was that he himself, with the help of four gentlemen who had since left Algiers, had arranged the whole, and that the sixty who were to accompany him were not to know anything of it until the last moment. Finding he could make nothing of him, the Dey sent him back to prison more heavily ironed than before.

The poverty-stricken Cervantes family had been all this time trying once more to raise the ransom money, and at last a sum of three hundred ducats was got together and entrusted to the Redemptorist Father Juan Gil, who was about to sail for Algiers. The Dey, however, demanded more than double the sum offered, and as his term of office had expired and he was about to sail for Constantinople, taking all his slaves with him, the case of Cervantes was critical. He was already on board heavily ironed, when the Dey at length agreed to reduce his demand by one-half, and Father Gil by borrowing was able to make up the amount, and on September 19, 1580, after a captivity of five years all but a week, Cervantes was at last set free. Before long he discovered that Blanco de Paz, who claimed to be an officer of the Inquisition, was now concocting on false evidence a charge of misconduct to be brought against him on his return to Spain. To checkmate him Cervantes drew up a series of twenty-five questions, covering the whole period of his captivity, upon which he requested Father Gil to take the depositions of credible witnesses before a notary. Eleven witnesses taken from among the principal captives in Algiers deposed to all the facts above stated and to a great deal more besides. There is something touching in the admiration, love, and gratitude we see struggling to find expression in the formal language of the notary, as they testify one after another to the good deeds of Cervantes, how he comforted and helped the weak-hearted, how he kept up their drooping courage, how he shared his poor purse with this deponent, and how "in him this deponent found father and mother."

On his return to Spain he found his old regiment about to march for Portugal to support Philip's claim to the crown, and utterly penniless now, had no choice but to rejoin it. He was in the expeditions to the Azores in 1582 and the following year, and on the conclusion of the war returned to Spain in the autumn of 1583, bringing with him the manuscript of his pastoral romance, the "Galatea," and probably also, to judge by internal evidence, that of the first portion of "Persiles and Sigismunda." He also brought back with him, his biographers assert, an infant daughter, the offspring of an amour, as some of them with great circumstantiality inform us, with a Lisbon lady of noble birth, whose name, however, as well as that of the street she lived in, they omit to mention. The sole foundation for all this is that in 1605 there certainly was living in the family of Cervantes a Dona Isabel de Saavedra, who is described in an official document as his natural daughter, and then twenty years of age.

With his crippled left hand promotion in the army was hopeless, now that Don John was dead and he had no one to press his claims and services, and for a man drawing on to forty life in the ranks was a dismal prospect; he had already a certain reputation as a poet; he made up his mind, therefore, to cast his lot with literature, and for a first venture committed his "Galatea" to the press. It was published, as Salva y Mallen shows conclusively, at Alcala, his own birth-place, in 1585 and no doubt helped to make his name more widely known, but certainly did not do him much good in any other way.

While it was going through the press, he married Dona Catalina de Palacios Salazar y Vozmediano, a lady of Esquivias near Madrid, and apparently a friend of the family, who brought him a fortune which may possibly have served to keep the wolf from the door, but if so, that was all. The drama had by this time outgrown market-place stages and strolling companies, and with his old love for it he naturally turned to it for a congenial employment. In about three years he wrote twenty or thirty plays, which he tells us were performed without any throwing of cucumbers or other missiles, and ran their course without any hisses, outcries, or disturbance. In other words, his plays were not bad enough to be hissed off the stage, but not good enough to hold their own upon it. Only two of them have been preserved, but as they happen to be two of the seven or eight he mentions with complacency, we may assume they are favourable specimens, and no one who reads the "Numancia" and the "Trato de Argel" will feel any surprise that they failed as acting dramas. Whatever merits they may have, whatever occasional they may show, they are, as regards construction, incurably clumsy. How completely they failed is manifest from the fact that with all his sanguine temperament and indomitable perseverance he was unable to maintain the struggle to gain a livelihood as a dramatist for more than three years; nor was the rising popularity of Lope the cause, as is often said, notwithstanding his own words to the contrary. When Lope began to write for the stage is uncertain, but it was certainly after Cervantes went to Seville.

Among the "Nuevos Documentos" printed by Senor Asensio y Toledo is one dated 1592, and curiously characteristic of Cervantes. It is an agreement with one Rodrigo Osorio, a manager, who was to accept six comedies at fifty ducats (about 6l.) apiece, not to be paid in any case unless it appeared on representation that the said comedy was one of the best that had ever been represented in Spain. The test does not seem to have been ever applied; perhaps it was sufficiently apparent to Rodrigo Osorio that the comedies were not among the best that had ever been represented. Among the correspondence of Cervantes there might have been found, no doubt, more than one letter like that we see in the "Rake's Progress," "Sir, I have read your play, and it will not doo."

He was more successful in a literary contest at Saragossa in 1595 in honour of the canonisation of St. Jacinto, when his composition won the first prize, three silver spoons. The year before this he had been appointed a collector of revenues for the kingdom of Granada. In order to remit the money he had collected more conveniently to the treasury, he entrusted it to a merchant, who failed and absconded; and as the bankrupt's assets were insufficient to cover the whole, he was sent to prison at Seville in September 1597. The balance against him, however, was a small one, about 26l., and on giving security for it he was released at the end of the year.

It was as he journeyed from town to town collecting the king's taxes, that he noted down those bits of inn and wayside life and character that abound in the pages of "Don Quixote:" the Benedictine monks with spectacles and sunshades, mounted on their tall mules; the strollers in costume bound for the next village; the barber with his basin on his head, on his way to bleed a patient; the recruit with his breeches in his bundle, tramping along the road singing; the reapers gathered in the venta gateway listening to "Felixmarte of Hircania" read out to them; and those little Hogarthian touches that he so well knew how to bring in, the ox-tail hanging up with the landlord's comb stuck in it, the wine-skins at the bed-head, and those notable examples of hostelry art, Helen going off in high spirits on Paris's arm, and Dido on the tower dropping tears as big as walnuts. Nay, it may well be that on those journeys into remote regions he came across now and then a specimen of the pauper gentleman, with his lean hack and his greyhound and his books of chivalry, dreaming away his life in happy ignorance that the world had changed since his great-grandfather's old helmet was new. But it was in Seville that he found out his true vocation, though he himself would not by any means have admitted it to be so. It was there, in Triana, that he was first tempted to try his hand at drawing from life, and first brought his humour into play in the exquisite little sketch of "Rinconete y Cortadillo," the germ, in more ways than one, of "Don Quixote."

Where and when that was written, we cannot tell. After his imprisonment all trace of Cervantes in his official capacity disappears, from which it may be inferred that he was not reinstated. That he was still in Seville in November 1598 appears from a satirical sonnet of his on the elaborate catafalque erected to testify the grief of the city at the death of Philip II, but from this up to 1603 we have no clue to his movements. The words in the preface to the First Part of "Don Quixote" are generally held to be conclusive that he conceived the idea of the book, and wrote the beginning of it at least, in a prison, and that he may have done so is extremely likely.

There is a tradition that Cervantes read some portions of his work to a select audience at the Duke of Bejar's, which may have helped to make the book known; but the obvious conclusion is that the First Part of "Don Quixote" lay on his hands some time before he could find a publisher bold enough to undertake a venture of so novel a character; and so little faith in it had Francisco Robles of Madrid, to whom at last he sold it, that he did not care to incur the expense of securing the copyright for Aragon or Portugal, contenting himself with that for Castile. The printing was finished in December, and the book came out with the new year, 1605. It is often said that "Don Quixote" was at first received coldly. The facts show just the contrary. No sooner was it in the hands of the public than preparations were made to issue pirated editions at Lisbon and Valencia, and to bring out a second edition with the additional copyrights for Aragon and Portugal, which he secured in February.

No doubt it was received with something more than coldness by certain sections of the community. Men of wit, taste, and discrimination among the aristocracy gave it a hearty welcome, but the aristocracy in general were not likely to relish a book that turned their favourite reading into ridicule and laughed at so many of their favourite ideas. The dramatists who gathered round Lope as their leader regarded Cervantes as their common enemy, and it is plain that he was equally obnoxious to the other clique, the culto poets who had Gongora for their chief. Navarrete, who knew nothing of the letter above mentioned, tries hard to show that the relations between Cervantes and Lope were of a very friendly sort, as indeed they were until "Don Quixote" was written. Cervantes, indeed, to the last generously and manfully declared his admiration of Lope's powers, his unfailing invention, and his marvellous fertility; but in the preface of the First Part of "Don Quixote" and in the verses of "Urganda the Unknown," and one or two other places, there are, if we read between the lines, sly hits at Lope's vanities and affectations that argue no personal good-will; and Lope openly sneers at "Don Quixote" and Cervantes, and fourteen years after his death gives him only a few lines of cold commonplace in the "Laurel de Apolo," that seem all the colder for the eulogies of a host of nonentities whose names are found nowhere else.

In 1601 Valladolid was made the seat of the Court, and at the beginning of 1603 Cervantes had been summoned thither in connection with the balance due by him to the Treasury, which was still outstanding. He remained at Valladolid, apparently supporting himself by agencies and scrivener's work of some sort; probably drafting petitions and drawing up statements of claims to be presented to the Council, and the like. So, at least, we gather from the depositions taken on the occasion of the death of a gentleman, the victim of a street brawl, who had been carried into the house in which he lived. In these he himself is described as a man who wrote and transacted business, and it appears that his household then consisted of his wife, the natural daughter Isabel de Saavedra already mentioned, his sister Andrea, now a widow, her daughter Constanza, a mysterious Magdalena de Sotomayor calling herself his sister, for whom his biographers cannot account, and a servant-maid.

Meanwhile "Don Quixote" had been growing in favour, and its author's name was now known beyond the Pyrenees. In 1607 an edition was printed at Brussels. Robles, the Madrid publisher, found it necessary to meet the demand by a third edition, the seventh in all, in 1608. The popularity of the book in Italy was such that a Milan bookseller was led to bring out an edition in 1610; and another was called for in Brussels in 1611. It might naturally have been expected that, with such proofs before him that he had hit the taste of the public, Cervantes would have at once set about redeeming his rather vague promise of a second volume.

But, to all appearance, nothing was farther from his thoughts. He had still by him one or two short tales of the same vintage as those he had inserted in "Don Quixote" and instead of continuing the adventures of Don Quixote, he set to work to write more of these "Novelas Exemplares" as he afterwards called them, with a view to making a book of them.

The novels were published in the summer of 1613, with a dedication to the Conde de Lemos, the Maecenas of the day, and with one of those chatty confidential prefaces Cervantes was so fond of. In this, eight years and a half after the First Part of "Don Quixote" had appeared, we get the first hint of a forthcoming Second Part. "You shall see shortly," he says, "the further exploits of Don Quixote and humours of Sancho Panza." His idea of "shortly" was a somewhat elastic one, for, as we know by the date to Sancho's letter, he had barely one-half of the book completed that time twelvemonth.

But more than poems, or pastorals, or novels, it was his dramatic ambition that engrossed his thoughts. The same indomitable spirit that kept him from despair in the bagnios of Algiers, and prompted him to attempt the escape of himself and his comrades again and again, made him persevere in spite of failure and discouragement in his efforts to win the ear of the public as a dramatist. The temperament of Cervantes was essentially sanguine. The portrait he draws in the preface to the novels, with the aquiline features, chestnut hair, smooth untroubled forehead, and bright cheerful eyes, is the very portrait of a sanguine man. Nothing that the managers might say could persuade him that the merits of his plays would not be recognised at last if they were only given a fair chance. The old soldier of the Spanish Salamis was bent on being the Aeschylus of Spain. He was to found a great national drama, based on the true principles of art, that was to be the envy of all nations; he was to drive from the stage the silly, childish plays, the "mirrors of nonsense and models of folly" that were in vogue through the cupidity of the managers and shortsightedness of the authors; he was to correct and educate the public taste until it was ripe for tragedies on the model of the Greek drama—like the "Numancia" for instance—and comedies that would not only amuse but improve and instruct. All this he was to do, could he once get a hearing: there was the initial difficulty.

He shows plainly enough, too, that "Don Quixote" and the demolition of the chivalry romances was not the work that lay next his heart. He was, indeed, as he says himself in his preface, more a stepfather than a father to "Don Quixote." Never was great work so neglected by its author. That it was written carelessly, hastily, and by fits and starts, was not always his fault, but it seems clear he never read what he sent to the press. He knew how the printers had blundered, but he never took the trouble to correct them when the third edition was in progress, as a man who really cared for the child of his brain would have done. He appears to have regarded the book as little more than a mere libro de entretenimiento, an amusing book, a thing, as he says in the "Viaje," "to divert the melancholy moody heart at any time or season." No doubt he had an affection for his hero, and was very proud of Sancho Panza. It would have been strange indeed if he had not been proud of the most humorous creation in all fiction. He was proud, too, of the popularity and success of the book, and beyond measure delightful is the naivete with which he shows his pride in a dozen passages in the Second Part. But it was not the success he coveted. In all probability he would have given all the success of "Don Quixote," nay, would have seen every copy of "Don Quixote" burned in the Plaza Mayor, for one such success as Lope de Vega was enjoying on an average once a week.

And so he went on, dawdling over "Don Quixote," adding a chapter now and again, and putting it aside to turn to "Persiles and Sigismunda"—which, as we know, was to be the most entertaining book in the language, and the rival of "Theagenes and Chariclea"—or finishing off one of his darling comedies; and if Robles asked when "Don Quixote" would be ready, the answer no doubt was: En breve—shortly, there was time enough for that. At sixty-eight he was as full of life and hope and plans for the future as a boy of eighteen.

Nemesis was coming, however. He had got as far as Chapter LIX, which at his leisurely pace he could hardly have reached before October or November 1614, when there was put into his hand a small octave lately printed at Tarragona, and calling itself "Second Volume of the Ingenious Gentleman Don Quixote of La Mancha: by the Licentiate Alonso Fernandez de Avellaneda of Tordesillas." The last half of Chapter LIX and most of the following chapters of the Second Part give us some idea of the effect produced upon him, and his irritation was not likely to be lessened by the reflection that he had no one to blame but himself. Had Avellaneda, in fact, been content with merely bringing out a continuation to "Don Quixote," Cervantes would have had no reasonable grievance. His own intentions were expressed in the very vaguest language at the end of the book; nay, in his last words, "forse altro cantera con miglior plettro," he seems actually to invite some one else to continue the work, and he made no sign until eight years and a half had gone by; by which time Avellaneda's volume was no doubt written.

In fact Cervantes had no case, or a very bad one, as far as the mere continuation was concerned. But Avellaneda chose to write a preface to it, full of such coarse personal abuse as only an ill-conditioned man could pour out. He taunts Cervantes with being old, with having lost his hand, with having been in prison, with being poor, with being friendless, accuses him of envy of Lope's success, of petulance and querulousness, and so on; and it was in this that the sting lay. Avellaneda's reason for this personal attack is obvious enough. Whoever he may have been, it is clear that he was one of the dramatists of Lope's school, for he has the impudence to charge Cervantes with attacking him as well as Lope in his criticism on the drama. His identification has exercised the best critics and baffled all the ingenuity and research that has been brought to bear on it. Navarrete and Ticknor both incline to the belief that Cervantes knew who he was; but I must say I think the anger he shows suggests an invisible assailant; it is like the irritation of a man stung by a mosquito in the dark. Cervantes from certain solecisms of language pronounces him to be an Aragonese, and Pellicer, an Aragonese himself, supports this view and believes him, moreover, to have been an ecclesiastic, a Dominican probably.

Any merit Avellaneda has is reflected from Cervantes, and he is too dull to reflect much. "Dull and dirty" will always be, I imagine, the verdict of the vast majority of unprejudiced readers. He is, at best, a poor plagiarist; all he can do is to follow slavishly the lead given him by Cervantes; his only humour lies in making Don Quixote take inns for castles and fancy himself some legendary or historical personage, and Sancho mistake words, invert proverbs, and display his gluttony; all through he shows a proclivity to coarseness and dirt, and he has contrived to introduce two tales filthier than anything by the sixteenth century novellieri and without their sprightliness.

But whatever Avellaneda and his book may be, we must not forget the debt we owe them. But for them, there can be no doubt, "Don Quixote" would have come to us a mere torso instead of a complete work. Even if Cervantes had finished the volume he had in hand, most assuredly he would have left off with a promise of a Third Part, giving the further adventures of Don Quixote and humours of Sancho Panza as shepherds. It is plain that he had at one time an intention of dealing with the pastoral romances as he had dealt with the books of chivalry, and but for Avellaneda he would have tried to carry it out. But it is more likely that, with his plans, and projects, and hopefulness, the volume would have remained unfinished till his death, and that we should have never made the acquaintance of the Duke and Duchess, or gone with Sancho to Barataria.

From the moment the book came into his hands he seems to have been haunted by the fear that there might be more Avellanedas in the field, and putting everything else aside, he set himself to finish off his task and protect Don Quixote in the only way he could, by killing him. The conclusion is no doubt a hasty and in some places clumsy piece of work and the frequent repetition of the scolding administered to Avellaneda becomes in the end rather wearisome; but it is, at any rate, a conclusion and for that we must thank Avellaneda.

The new volume was ready for the press in February, but was not printed till the very end of 1615, and during the interval Cervantes put together the comedies and interludes he had written within the last few years, and, as he adds plaintively, found no demand for among the managers, and published them with a preface, worth the book it introduces tenfold, in which he gives an account of the early Spanish stage, and of his own attempts as a dramatist. It is needless to say they were put forward by Cervantes in all good faith and full confidence in their merits. The reader, however, was not to suppose they were his last word or final effort in the drama, for he had in hand a comedy called "Engano a los ojos," about which, if he mistook not, there would be no question.

Of this dramatic masterpiece the world has no opportunity of judging; his health had been failing for some time, and he died, apparently of dropsy, on the 23rd of April, 1616, the day on which England lost Shakespeare, nominally at least, for the English calendar had not yet been reformed. He died as he had lived, accepting his lot bravely and cheerfully.

Was it an unhappy life, that of Cervantes? His biographers all tell us that it was; but I must say I doubt it. It was a hard life, a life of poverty, of incessant struggle, of toil ill paid, of disappointment, but Cervantes carried within himself the antidote to all these evils. His was not one of those light natures that rise above adversity merely by virtue of their own buoyancy; it was in the fortitude of a high spirit that he was proof against it. It is impossible to conceive Cervantes giving way to despondency or prostrated by dejection. As for poverty, it was with him a thing to be laughed over, and the only sigh he ever allows to escape him is when he says, "Happy he to whom Heaven has given a piece of bread for which he is not bound to give thanks to any but Heaven itself." Add to all this his vital energy and mental activity, his restless invention and his sanguine temperament, and there will be reason enough to doubt whether his could have been a very unhappy life. He who could take Cervantes' distresses together with his apparatus for enduring them would not make so bad a bargain, perhaps, as far as happiness in life is concerned.

Of his burial-place nothing is known except that he was buried, in accordance with his will, in the neighbouring convent of Trinitarian nuns, of which it is supposed his daughter, Isabel de Saavedra, was an inmate, and that a few years afterwards the nuns removed to another convent, carrying their dead with them. But whether the remains of Cervantes were included in the removal or not no one knows, and the clue to their resting-place is now lost beyond all hope. This furnishes perhaps the least defensible of the items in the charge of neglect brought against his contemporaries. In some of the others there is a good deal of exaggeration. To listen to most of his biographers one would suppose that all Spain was in league not only against the man but against his memory, or at least that it was insensible to his merits, and left him to live in misery and die of want. To talk of his hard life and unworthy employments in Andalusia is absurd. What had he done to distinguish him from thousands of other struggling men earning a precarious livelihood? True, he was a gallant soldier, who had been wounded and had undergone captivity and suffering in his country's cause, but there were hundreds of others in the same case. He had written a mediocre specimen of an insipid class of romance, and some plays which manifestly did not comply with the primary condition of pleasing: were the playgoers to patronise plays that did not amuse them, because the author was to produce "Don Quixote" twenty years afterwards?

The scramble for copies which, as we have seen, followed immediately on the appearance of the book, does not look like general insensibility to its merits. No doubt it was received coldly by some, but if a man writes a book in ridicule of periwigs he must make his account with being coldly received by the periwig wearers and hated by the whole tribe of wigmakers. If Cervantes had the chivalry-romance readers, the sentimentalists, the dramatists, and the poets of the period all against him, it was because "Don Quixote" was what it was; and if the general public did not come forward to make him comfortable for the rest of his days, it is no more to be charged with neglect and ingratitude than the English-speaking public that did not pay off Scott's liabilities. It did the best it could; it read his book and liked it and bought it, and encouraged the bookseller to pay him well for others.

It has been also made a reproach to Spain that she has erected no monument to the man she is proudest of; no monument, that is to say, of him; for the bronze statue in the little garden of the Plaza de las Cortes, a fair work of art no doubt, and unexceptionable had it been set up to the local poet in the market-place of some provincial town, is not worthy of Cervantes or of Madrid. But what need has Cervantes of "such weak witness of his name;" or what could a monument do in his case except testify to the self-glorification of those who had put it up? Si monumentum quoeris, circumspice. The nearest bookseller's shop will show what bathos there would be in a monument to the author of "Don Quixote."

Nine editions of the First Part of "Don Quixote" had already appeared before Cervantes died, thirty thousand copies in all, according to his own estimate, and a tenth was printed at Barcelona the year after his death. So large a number naturally supplied the demand for some time, but by 1634 it appears to have been exhausted; and from that time down to the present day the stream of editions has continued to flow rapidly and regularly. The translations show still more clearly in what request the book has been from the very outset. In seven years from the completion of the work it had been translated into the four leading languages of Europe. Except the Bible, in fact, no book has been so widely diffused as "Don Quixote." The "Imitatio Christi" may have been translated into as many different languages, and perhaps "Robinson Crusoe" and the "Vicar of Wakefield" into nearly as many, but in multiplicity of translations and editions "Don Quixote" leaves them all far behind.

Still more remarkable is the character of this wide diffusion. "Don Quixote" has been thoroughly naturalised among people whose ideas about knight-errantry, if they had any at all, were of the vaguest, who had never seen or heard of a book of chivalry, who could not possibly feel the humour of the burlesque or sympathise with the author's purpose. Another curious fact is that this, the most cosmopolitan book in the world, is one of the most intensely national. "Manon Lescaut" is not more thoroughly French, "Tom Jones" not more English, "Rob Roy" not more Scotch, than "Don Quixote" is Spanish, in character, in ideas, in sentiment, in local colour, in everything. What, then, is the secret of this unparalleled popularity, increasing year by year for well-nigh three centuries? One explanation, no doubt, is that of all the books in the world, "Don Quixote" is the most catholic. There is something in it for every sort of reader, young or old, sage or simple, high or low. As Cervantes himself says with a touch of pride, "It is thumbed and read and got by heart by people of all sorts; the children turn its leaves, the young people read it, the grown men understand it, the old folk praise it."

But it would be idle to deny that the ingredient which, more than its humour, or its wisdom, or the fertility of invention or knowledge of human nature it displays, has insured its success with the multitude, is the vein of farce that runs through it. It was the attack upon the sheep, the battle with the wine-skins, Mambrino's helmet, the balsam of Fierabras, Don Quixote knocked over by the sails of the windmill, Sancho tossed in the blanket, the mishaps and misadventures of master and man, that were originally the great attraction, and perhaps are so still to some extent with the majority of readers. It is plain that "Don Quixote" was generally regarded at first, and indeed in Spain for a long time, as little more than a queer droll book, full of laughable incidents and absurd situations, very amusing, but not entitled to much consideration or care. All the editions printed in Spain from 1637 to 1771, when the famous printer Ibarra took it up, were mere trade editions, badly and carelessly printed on vile paper and got up in the style of chap-books intended only for popular use, with, in most instances, uncouth illustrations and clap-trap additions by the publisher.

To England belongs the credit of having been the first country to recognise the right of "Don Quixote" to better treatment than this. The London edition of 1738, commonly called Lord Carteret's from having been suggested by him, was not a mere edition de luxe. It produced "Don Quixote" in becoming form as regards paper and type, and embellished with plates which, if not particularly happy as illustrations, were at least well intentioned and well executed, but it also aimed at correctness of text, a matter to which nobody except the editors of the Valencia and Brussels editions had given even a passing thought; and for a first attempt it was fairly successful, for though some of its emendations are inadmissible, a good many of them have been adopted by all subsequent editors.

The zeal of publishers, editors, and annotators brought about a remarkable change of sentiment with regard to "Don Quixote." A vast number of its admirers began to grow ashamed of laughing over it. It became almost a crime to treat it as a humorous book. The humour was not entirely denied, but, according to the new view, it was rated as an altogether secondary quality, a mere accessory, nothing more than the stalking-horse under the presentation of which Cervantes shot his philosophy or his satire, or whatever it was he meant to shoot; for on this point opinions varied. All were agreed, however, that the object he aimed at was not the books of chivalry. He said emphatically in the preface to the First Part and in the last sentence of the Second, that he had no other object in view than to discredit these books, and this, to advanced criticism, made it clear that his object must have been something else.

One theory was that the book was a kind of allegory, setting forth the eternal struggle between the ideal and the real, between the spirit of poetry and the spirit of prose; and perhaps German philosophy never evolved a more ungainly or unlikely camel out of the depths of its inner consciousness. Something of the antagonism, no doubt, is to be found in "Don Quixote," because it is to be found everywhere in life, and Cervantes drew from life. It is difficult to imagine a community in which the never-ceasing game of cross-purposes between Sancho Panza and Don

Quixote would not be recognized as true to nature. In the stone age, among the lake dwellers, among the cave men, there were Don Quixotes and Sancho Panzas; there must have been the troglodyte who never could see the facts before his eyes, and the troglodyte who could see nothing else. But to suppose Cervantes deliberately setting himself to expound any such idea in two stout quarto volumes is to suppose something not only very unlike the age in which he lived, but altogether unlike Cervantes himself, who would have been the first to laugh at an attempt of the sort made by anyone else.

The extraordinary influence of the romances of chivalry in his day is quite enough to account for the genesis of the book. Some idea of the prodigious development of this branch of literature in the sixteenth century may be obtained from the scrutiny of Chapter VII, if the reader bears in mind that only a portion of the romances belonging to by far the largest group are enumerated. As to its effect upon the nation, there is abundant evidence. From the time when the Amadises and Palmerins began to grow popular down to the very end of the century, there is a steady stream of invective, from men whose character and position lend weight to their words, against the romances of chivalry and the infatuation of their readers. Ridicule was the only besom to sweep away that dust.

That this was the task Cervantes set himself, and that he had ample provocation to urge him to it, will be sufficiently clear to those who look into the evidence; as it will be also that it was not chivalry itself that he attacked and swept away. Of all the absurdities that, thanks to poetry, will be repeated to the end of time, there is no greater one than saying that "Cervantes smiled Spain's chivalry away." In the first place there was no chivalry for him to smile away. Spain's chivalry had been dead for more than a century. Its work was done when Granada fell, and as chivalry was essentially republican in its nature, it could not live under the rule that Ferdinand substituted for the free institutions of mediaeval Spain. What he did smile away was not chivalry but a degrading mockery of it.

The true nature of the "right arm" and the "bright array," before which, according to the poet, "the world gave ground," and which Cervantes' single laugh demolished, may be gathered from the words of one of his own countrymen, Don Felix Pacheco, as reported by Captain George Carleton, in his "Military Memoirs from 1672 to 1713." "Before the appearance in the world of that labour of Cervantes," he said, "it was next to an impossibility for a man to walk the streets with any delight or without danger. There were seen so many cavaliers prancing and curvetting before the windows of their mistresses, that a stranger would have imagined the whole nation to have been nothing less than a race of knight-errants. But after the world became a little acquainted with that notable history, the man that was seen in that once celebrated drapery was pointed at as a Don Quixote, and found himself the jest of high and low. And I verily believe that to this, and this only, we owe that dampness and poverty of spirit which has run through all our councils for a century past, so little agreeable to those nobler actions of our famous ancestors."

To call "Don Quixote" a sad book, preaching a pessimist view of life, argues a total misconception of its drift. It would be so if its moral were that, in this world, true enthusiasm naturally leads to ridicule and discomfiture. But it preaches nothing of the sort; its moral, so far as it can be said to have one, is that the spurious enthusiasm that is born of vanity and self-conceit, that is made an end in itself, not a means to an end, that acts on mere impulse, regardless of circumstances and consequences, is mischievous to its owner, and a very considerable nuisance to the community at large. To those who cannot distinguish between the one kind and the other, no doubt "Don Quixote" is a sad book; no doubt to some minds it is very sad that a man who had just uttered so beautiful a sentiment as that "it is a hard case to make slaves of those whom God and Nature made free," should be ungratefully pelted by the scoundrels his crazy philanthropy had let loose on society; but to others of a more judicial cast it will be a matter of regret that reckless self-sufficient enthusiasm is not oftener requited in some such way for all the mischief it does in the world.

A very slight examination of the structure of "Don Quixote" will suffice to show that Cervantes had no deep design or elaborate plan in his mind when he began the book. When he wrote those lines in which "with a few strokes of a great master he sets before us the pauper gentleman," he had no idea of the goal to which his imagination was leading him. There can be little doubt that all he contemplated was a short tale to range with those he had already written, a tale setting forth the ludicrous results that might be expected to follow the attempt of a crazy gentleman to act the part of a knight-errant in modern life.

It is plain, for one thing, that Sancho Panza did not enter into the original scheme, for had Cervantes thought of him he certainly would not have omitted him in his hero's outfit, which he obviously meant to be complete. Him we owe to the landlord's chance remark in Chapter III that knights seldom travelled without squires. To try to think of a Don Quixote without Sancho Panza is like trying to think of a one-bladed pair of scissors.

The story was written at first, like the others, without any division and without the intervention of Cide Hamete Benengeli; and it seems not unlikely that Cervantes had some intention of bringing Dulcinea, or Aldonza Lorenzo, on the scene in person. It was probably the ransacking of the Don's library and the discussion on the books of chivalry that first suggested it to him that his idea was capable of development. What, if instead of a mere string of farcical misadventures, he were to make his tale a burlesque of one of these books, caricaturing their style, incidents, and spirit?

In pursuance of this change of plan, he hastily and somewhat clumsily divided what he had written into chapters on the model of "Amadis," invented the fable of a mysterious Arabic manuscript, and set up Cide Hamete Benengeli in imitation of the almost invariable practice of the chivalry-romance authors, who were fond of tracing their books to some recondite source. In working out the new ideas, he soon found the value of Sancho Panza. Indeed, the keynote, not only to Sancho's part, but to the whole book, is struck in the first words Sancho utters when he announces his intention of taking his ass with him. "About the ass," we are told, "Don Quixote hesitated a little, trying whether he could call to mind any knight-errant taking with him an esquire mounted on ass-back; but no instance occurred to his memory." We can see the whole scene at a glance, the stolid unconsciousness of Sancho and the perplexity of his master, upon whose perception the incongruity has just forced itself. This is Sancho's mission throughout the book; he is an unconscious Mephistopheles, always unwittingly making mockery of his master's aspirations, always exposing the fallacy of his ideas by some unintentional ad absurdum, always bringing him back to the world of fact and commonplace by force of sheer stolidity.

By the time Cervantes had got his volume of novels off his hands, and summoned up resolution enough to set about the Second Part in earnest, the case was very much altered. Don Quixote and Sancho Panza had not merely found favour, but had already become, what they have never since ceased to be, veritable entities to the popular imagination. There was no occasion for him now to interpolate extraneous matter; nay, his readers told him plainly that what they wanted of him was more Don Quixote and more Sancho Panza, and not novels, tales, or digressions. To himself, too, his creations had become realities, and he had become proud of them, especially of Sancho. He began the Second Part, therefore, under very different conditions, and the difference makes itself manifest at once. Even in translation the style will be seen to be far easier, more flowing, more natural, and more like that of a man sure of himself and of his audience. Don Quixote and Sancho undergo a change also. In the First Part, Don Quixote has no character or individuality whatever. He is nothing more than a crazy representative of the sentiments of the chivalry romances. In all that he says and does he is simply repeating the lesson he has learned from his books; and therefore, it is absurd to speak of him in the gushing strain of the sentimental critics when they dilate upon his nobleness, disinterestedness, dauntless courage, and so forth. It was the business of a knight-errant to right wrongs, redress injuries, and succour the distressed, and this, as a matter of course, he makes his business when he takes up the part; a knight-errant was bound to be intrepid, and so he feels bound to cast fear aside. Of all Byron's melodious nonsense about Don Quixote, the most nonsensical statement is that "'t is his virtue makes him mad!" The exact opposite is the truth; it is his madness makes him virtuous.

In the Second Part, Cervantes repeatedly reminds the reader, as if it was a point upon which he was anxious there should be no mistake, that his hero's madness is strictly confined to delusions on the subject of chivalry, and that on every other subject he is discreto, one, in fact, whose faculty of discernment is in perfect order. The advantage of this is that he is enabled to make use of Don Quixote as a mouthpiece for his own reflections, and so, without seeming to digress, allow himself the relief of digression when he requires it, as freely as in a commonplace book.

It is true the amount of individuality bestowed upon Don Quixote is not very great. There are some natural touches of character about him, such as his mixture of irascibility and placability, and his curious affection for Sancho together with his impatience of the squire's loquacity and impertinence; but in the main, apart from his craze, he is little more than a thoughtful, cultured gentleman, with instinctive good taste and a great deal of shrewdness and originality of mind.

As to Sancho, it is plain, from the concluding words of the preface to the First Part, that he was a favourite with his creator even before he had been taken into favour by the public. An inferior genius, taking him in hand a second time, would very likely have tried to improve him by making him more comical, clever, amiable, or virtuous. But Cervantes was too true an artist to spoil his work in this way. Sancho, when he reappears, is the old Sancho with the old familiar features; but with a difference; they have been brought out more distinctly, but at the same time with a careful avoidance of anything like caricature; the outline has been filled in where filling in was necessary, and, vivified by a few touches of a master's hand, Sancho stands before us as he might in a character portrait by Velazquez. He is a much more important and prominent figure in the Second Part than in the First; indeed, it is his matchless mendacity about Dulcinea that to a great extent supplies the action of the story.

His development in this respect is as remarkable as in any other. In the First Part he displays a great natural gift of lying. His lies are not of the highly imaginative sort that liars in fiction commonly indulge in; like Falstaff's, they resemble the father that begets them; they are simple, homely, plump lies; plain working lies, in short. But in the service of such a master as Don Quixote he develops rapidly, as we see when he comes to palm off the three country wenches as Dulcinea and her ladies in waiting. It is worth noticing how, flushed by his success in this instance, he is tempted afterwards to try a flight beyond his powers in his account of the journey on Clavileno.

In the Second Part it is the spirit rather than the incidents of the chivalry romances that is the subject of the burlesque. Enchantments of the sort travestied in those of Dulcinea and the Trifaldi and the cave of Montesinos play a leading part in the later and inferior romances, and another distinguishing feature is caricatured in Don Quixote's blind adoration of Dulcinea. In the romances of chivalry love is either a mere animalism or a fantastic idolatry. Only a coarse-minded man would care to make merry with the former, but to one of Cervantes' humour the latter was naturally an attractive subject for ridicule. Like everything else in these romances, it is a gross exaggeration of the real sentiment of chivalry, but its peculiar extravagance is probably due to the influence of those masters of hyperbole, the Provencal poets. When a troubadour professed his readiness to obey his lady in all things, he made it incumbent upon the next comer, if he wished to avoid the imputation of tameness and commonplace, to declare himself the slave of her will, which the next was compelled to cap by some still stronger declaration; and so expressions of devotion went on rising one above the other like biddings at an auction, and a conventional language of gallantry and theory of love came into being that in time permeated the literature of Southern Europe, and bore fruit, in one direction in the transcendental worship of Beatrice and Laura, and in another in the grotesque idolatry which found exponents in writers like Feliciano de Silva. This is what Cervantes deals with in Don Quixote's passion for Dulcinea, and in no instance has he carried out the burlesque more happily. By keeping Dulcinea in the background, and making her a vague shadowy being of whose very existence we are left in doubt, he invests Don Quixote's worship of her virtues and charms with an additional extravagance, and gives still more point to the caricature of the sentiment and language of the romances.

One of the great merits of "Don Quixote," and one of the qualities that have secured its acceptance by all classes of readers and made it the most cosmopolitan of books, is its simplicity. There are, of course, points obvious enough to a Spanish seventeenth century audience which do not immediately strike a reader now-a-days, and Cervantes often takes it for granted that an allusion will be generally understood which is only intelligible to a few. For example, on many of his readers in Spain, and most of his readers out of it, the significance of his choice of a country for his hero is completely lost. It would be going too far to say that no one can thoroughly comprehend "Don Quixote" without having seen La Mancha, but undoubtedly even a glimpse of La Mancha will give an insight into the meaning of Cervantes such as no commentator can give. Of all the regions of Spain it is the last that would suggest the idea of romance. Of all the dull central plateau of the Peninsula it is the dullest tract. There is something impressive about the grim solitudes of Estremadura; and if the plains of Leon and Old Castile are bald and dreary, they are studded with old cities renowned in history and rich in relics of the past. But there is no redeeming feature in the Manchegan landscape; it has all the sameness of the desert without its dignity; the few towns and villages that break its monotony are mean and commonplace, there is nothing venerable about them, they have not even the picturesqueness of poverty; indeed, Don Quixote's own village, Argamasilla, has a sort of oppressive respectability in the prim regularity of its streets and houses; everything is ignoble; the very windmills are the ugliest and shabbiest of the windmill kind.

To anyone who knew the country well, the mere style and title of "Don Quixote of La Mancha" gave the key to the author's meaning at once. La Mancha as the knight's country and scene of his chivalries is of a piece with the pasteboard helmet, the farm-labourer on ass-back for a squire, knighthood conferred by a rascally ventero, convicts taken for victims of oppression, and the rest of the incongruities between Don Quixote's world and the world he lived in, between things as he saw them and things as they were.

It is strange that this element of incongruity, underlying the whole humour and purpose of the book, should have been so little heeded by the majority of those who have undertaken to interpret "Don Quixote." It has been completely overlooked, for example, by the illustrators. To be sure, the great majority of the artists who illustrated "Don Quixote" knew nothing whatever of Spain. To them a venta conveyed no idea but the abstract one of a roadside inn, and they could not therefore do full justice to the humour of Don Quixote's misconception in taking it for a castle, or perceive the remoteness of all its realities from his ideal. But even when better informed they seem to have no apprehension of the full force of the discrepancy. Take, for instance, Gustave Dore's drawing of Don Quixote watching his armour in the inn-yard. Whether or not the Venta de Quesada on the Seville road is, as tradition maintains, the inn described in "Don Quixote," beyond all question it was just such an inn-yard as the one behind it that Cervantes had in his mind's eye, and it was on just such a rude stone trough as that beside the primitive draw-well in the corner that he meant Don Quixote to deposit his armour. Gustave Dore makes it an elaborate fountain such as no arriero ever watered his mules at in the corral of any venta in Spain, and thereby entirely misses the point aimed at by Cervantes. It is the mean, prosaic, commonplace character of all the surroundings and circumstances that gives a significance to Don Quixote's vigil and the ceremony that follows.

Cervantes' humour is for the most part of that broader and simpler sort, the strength of which lies in the perception of the incongruous. It is the incongruity of Sancho in all his ways, words, and works, with the ideas and aims of his master, quite as much as the wonderful vitality and truth to nature of the character, that makes him the most humorous creation in the whole range of fiction. That unsmiling gravity of which Cervantes was the first great master, "Cervantes' serious air," which sits naturally on Swift alone, perhaps, of later humourists, is essential to this kind of humour, and here again Cervantes has suffered at the hands of his interpreters. Nothing, unless indeed the coarse buffoonery of Phillips, could be more out of place in an attempt to represent Cervantes, than a flippant, would-be facetious style, like that of Motteux's version for example, or the sprightly, jaunty air, French translators sometimes adopt. It is the grave matter-of-factness of the narrative, and the apparent unconsciousness of the author that he is saying anything ludicrous, anything but the merest commonplace, that give its peculiar flavour to the humour of Cervantes. His, in fact, is the exact opposite of the humour of Sterne and the self-conscious humourists. Even when Uncle Toby is at his best, you are always aware of "the man Sterne" behind him, watching you over his shoulder to see what effect he is producing. Cervantes always leaves you alone with Don Quixote and Sancho. He and Swift and the great humourists always keep themselves out of sight, or, more properly speaking, never think about themselves at all, unlike our latter-day school of humourists, who seem to have revived the old horse-collar method, and try to raise a laugh by some grotesque assumption of ignorance, imbecility, or bad taste.

It is true that to do full justice to Spanish humour in any other language is well-nigh an impossibility. There is a natural gravity and a sonorous stateliness about Spanish, be it ever so colloquial, that make an absurdity doubly absurd, and give plausibility to the most preposterous statement. This is what makes Sancho Panza's drollery the despair of the conscientious translator. Sancho's curt comments can never fall flat, but they lose half their flavour when transferred from their native Castilian into any other medium. But if foreigners have failed to do justice to the humour of Cervantes, they are no worse than his own countrymen. Indeed, were it not for the Spanish peasant's relish of "Don Quixote," one might be tempted to think that the great humourist was not looked upon as a humourist at all in his own country.

The craze of Don Quixote seems, in some instances, to have communicated itself to his critics, making them see things that are not in the book and run full tilt at phantoms that have no existence save in their own imaginations. Like a good many critics now-a-days, they forget that screams are not criticism, and that it is only vulgar tastes that are influenced by strings of superlatives, three-piled hyperboles, and pompous epithets. But what strikes one as particularly strange is that while they deal in extravagant eulogies, and ascribe all manner of imaginary ideas and qualities to Cervantes, they show no perception of the quality that ninety-nine out of a hundred of his readers would rate highest in him, and hold to be the one that raises him above all rivalry.

To speak of "Don Quixote" as if it were merely a humorous book would be a manifest misdescription. Cervantes at times makes it a kind of commonplace book for occasional essays and criticisms, or for the observations and reflections and gathered wisdom of a long and stirring life. It is a mine of shrewd observation on mankind and human nature. Among modern novels there may be, here and there, more elaborate studies of character, but there is no book richer in individualised character. What Coleridge said of Shakespeare in minimis is true of Cervantes; he never, even for the most temporary purpose, puts forward a lay figure. There is life and individuality in all his characters, however little they may have to do, or however short a time they may be before the reader. Samson Carrasco, the curate, Teresa Panza, Altisidora, even the two students met on the road to the cave of Montesinos, all live and move and have their being; and it is characteristic of the broad humanity of Cervantes that there is not a hateful one among them all. Even poor Maritornes, with her deplorable morals, has a kind heart of her own and "some faint and distant resemblance to a Christian about her;" and as for Sancho, though on dissection we fail to find a lovable trait in him, unless it be a sort of dog-like affection for his master, who is there that in his heart does not love him?

But it is, after all, the humour of "Don Quixote" that distinguishes it from all other books of the romance kind. It is this that makes it, as one of the most judicial-minded of modern critics calls it, "the best novel in the world beyond all comparison." It is its varied humour, ranging from broad farce to comedy as subtle as Shakespeare's or Moliere's that has naturalised it in every country where there are readers, and made it a classic in every language that has a literature.

DEDICATION OF PART I

TO THE DUKE OF BEJAR, MARQUIS OF GIBRALEON, COUNT OF BENALCAZAR
AND BANARES, VICECOUNT OF THE PUEBLA DE ALCOCER, MASTER OF THE
TOWNS OF CAPILLA, CURIEL AND BURGUILLOS

In belief of the good reception and honours that Your Excellency bestows on all sort of books,
as prince so inclined to favor good arts, chiefly those who by their nobleness do not submit to the
service and bribery of the vulgar, I have determined bringing to light The Ingenious Gentleman
Don Quixote of la Mancha, in shelter of Your Excellency's glamorous name, to whom, with the
obeisance I owe to such grandeur, I pray to receive it agreeably under his protection, so that in
this shadow, though deprived of that precious ornament of elegance and erudition that clothe the
works composed in the houses of those who know, it dares appear with assurance in the
judgment of some who, trespassing the bounds of their own ignorance, use to condemn with
more rigour and less justice the writings of others. It is my earnest hope that Your Excellency's
good counsel in regard to my honourable purpose, will not disdain the littleness of so humble a
service.

Miguel de Cervantes

e00.jpg (24K)

CHAPTER I.: WHICH TREATS OF THE CHARACTER AND PURSUITS OF THE FAMOUS GENTLEMAN DON QUIXOTE OF LA MANCHA

p007.jpg (150K)

In a village of La Mancha, the name of which I have no desire to call to mind, there lived not long since one of those gentlemen that keep a lance in the lance-rack, an old buckler, a lean hack, and a greyhound for coursing. An olla of rather more beef than mutton, a salad on most nights, scraps on Saturdays, lentils on Fridays, and a pigeon or so extra on Sundays, made away with three-quarters of his income. The rest of it went in a doublet of fine cloth and velvet breeches and shoes to match for holidays, while on week-days he made a brave figure in his best homespun. He had in his house a housekeeper past forty, a niece under twenty, and a lad for the field and market-place, who used to saddle the hack as well as handle the bill-hook. The age of this gentleman of ours was bordering on fifty; he was of a hardy habit, spare, gaunt-featured, a very early riser and a great sportsman. They will have it his surname was Quixada or Quesada (for here there is some difference of opinion among the authors who write on the subject), although from reasonable conjectures it seems plain that he was called Quexana. This, however, is of but little importance to our tale; it will be enough not to stray a hair's breadth from the truth in the telling of it.

You must know, then, that the above-named gentleman whenever he was at leisure (which was mostly all the year round) gave himself up to reading books of chivalry with such ardour and avidity that he almost entirely neglected the pursuit of his field-sports, and even the management of his property; and to such a pitch did his eagerness and infatuation go that he sold many an acre of tillageland to buy books of chivalry to read, and brought home as many of them as he could get. But of all there were none he liked so well as those of the famous Feliciano de Silva's composition, for their lucidity of style and complicated conceits were as pearls in his sight, particularly when in his reading he came upon courtships and cartels, where he often found passages like "the reason of the unreason with which my reason is afflicted so weakens my reason that with reason I murmur at your beauty;" or again, "the high heavens, that of your divinity divinely fortify you with the stars, render you deserving of the desert your greatness deserves." Over conceits of this sort the poor gentleman lost his wits, and used to lie awake striving to understand them and worm the meaning out of them; what Aristotle himself could not have made out or extracted had he come to life again for that special purpose. He was not at all easy about the wounds which Don Belianis gave and took, because it seemed to him that, great as were the surgeons who had cured him, he must have had his face and body covered all over with seams and scars. He commended, however, the author's way of ending his book with the promise of that interminable adventure, and many a time was he tempted to take up his pen and finish it properly as is there proposed, which no doubt he would have done, and made a successful piece of work of it too, had not greater and more absorbing thoughts prevented him.

Many an argument did he have with the curate of his village (a learned man, and a graduate of Siguenza) as to which had been the better knight, Palmerin of England or Amadis of Gaul.

Master Nicholas, the village barber, however, used to say that neither of them came up to the Knight of Phoebus, and that if there was any that could compare with him it was Don Galaor, the brother of Amadis of Gaul, because he had a spirit that was equal to every occasion, and was no finikin knight, nor lachrymose like his brother, while in the matter of valour he was not a whit behind him. In short, he became so absorbed in his books that he spent his nights from sunset to sunrise, and his days from dawn to dark, poring over them; and what with little sleep and much reading his brains got so dry that he lost his wits. His fancy grew full of what he used to read about in his books, enchantments, quarrels, battles, challenges, wounds, wooings, loves, agonies, and all sorts of impossible nonsense; and it so possessed his mind that the whole fabric of invention and fancy he read of was true, that to him no history in the world had more reality in it. He used to say the Cid Ruy Diaz was a very good knight, but that he was not to be compared with the Knight of the Burning Sword who with one back-stroke cut in half two fierce and monstrous giants. He thought more of Bernardo del Carpio because at Roncesvalles he slew Roland in spite of enchantments, availing himself of the artifice of Hercules when he strangled Antaeus the son of Terra in his arms. He approved highly of the giant Morgante, because, although of the giant breed which is always arrogant and ill-conditioned, he alone was affable and well-bred. But above all he admired Reinaldos of Montalban, especially when he saw him sallying forth from his castle and robbing everyone he met, and when beyond the seas he stole that image of Mahomet which, as his history says, was entirely of gold. To have a bout of kicking at that traitor of a Ganelon he would have given his housekeeper, and his niece into the bargain.

In short, his wits being quite gone, he hit upon the strangest notion that ever madman in this world hit upon, and that was that he fancied it was right and requisite, as well for the support of his own honour as for the service of his country, that he should make a knight-errant of himself, roaming the world over in full armour and on horseback in quest of adventures, and putting in practice himself all that he had read of as being the usual practices of knights-errant; righting every kind of wrong, and exposing himself to peril and danger from which, in the issue, he was to reap eternal renown and fame. Already the poor man saw himself crowned by the might of his arm Emperor of Trebizond at least; and so, led away by the intense enjoyment he found in these pleasant fancies, he set himself forthwith to put his scheme into execution.

The first thing he did was to clean up some armour that had belonged to his great-grandfather, and had been for ages lying forgotten in a corner eaten with rust and covered with mildew. He scoured and polished it as best he could, but he perceived one great defect in it, that it had no closed helmet, nothing but a simple morion. This deficiency, however, his ingenuity supplied, for he contrived a kind of half-helmet of pasteboard which, fitted on to the morion, looked like a whole one. It is true that, in order to see if it was strong and fit to stand a cut, he drew his sword and gave it a couple of slashes, the first of which undid in an instant what had taken him a week to do. The ease with which he had knocked it to pieces disconcerted him somewhat, and to guard against that danger he set to work again, fixing bars of iron on the inside until he was satisfied with its strength; and then, not caring to try any more experiments with it, he passed it and adopted it as a helmet of the most perfect construction.

He next proceeded to inspect his hack, which, with more quartos than a real and more blemishes than the steed of Gonela, that "tantum pellis et ossa fuit," surpassed in his eyes the Bucephalus of Alexander or the Babieca of the Cid. Four days were spent in thinking what name to give him, because (as he said to himself) it was not right that a horse belonging to a knight so famous, and one with such merits of his own, should be without some distinctive name, and he strove to adapt it so as to indicate what he had been before belonging to a knight-errant, and what he then was; for it was only reasonable that, his master taking a new character, he should take a new name, and that it should be a distinguished and full-sounding one, befitting the new order and calling he was about to follow. And so, after having composed, struck out, rejected, added to, unmade, and remade a multitude of names out of his memory and fancy, he decided upon calling him Rocinante, a name, to his thinking, lofty, sonorous, and significant of his condition as a hack before he became what he now was, the first and foremost of all the hacks in the world.

Having got a name for his horse so much to his taste, he was anxious to get one for himself, and he was eight days more pondering over this point, till at last he made up his mind to call himself "Don Quixote," whence, as has been already said, the authors of this veracious history have inferred that his name must have been beyond a doubt Quixada, and not Quesada as others would have it. Recollecting, however, that the valiant Amadis was not content to call himself curtly Amadis and nothing more, but added the name of his kingdom and country to make it famous, and called himself Amadis of Gaul, he, like a good knight, resolved to add on the name of his, and to style himself Don Quixote of La Mancha, whereby, he considered, he described accurately his origin and country, and did honour to it in taking his surname from it.

So then, his armour being furbished, his morion turned into a helmet, his hack christened, and he himself confirmed, he came to the conclusion that nothing more was needed now but to look out for a lady to be in love with; for a knight-errant without love was like a tree without leaves or fruit, or a body without a soul. As he said to himself, "If, for my sins, or by my good fortune, I come across some giant hereabouts, a common occurrence with knights-errant, and overthrow him in one onslaught, or cleave him asunder to the waist, or, in short, vanquish and subdue him, will it not be well to have some one I may send him to as a present, that he may come in and fall on his knees before my sweet lady, and in a humble, submissive voice say, 'I am the giant Caraculiambro, lord of the island of Malindrania, vanquished in single combat by the never sufficiently extolled knight Don Quixote of La Mancha, who has commanded me to present myself before your Grace, that your Highness dispose of me at your pleasure'?" Oh, how our good gentleman enjoyed the delivery of this speech, especially when he had thought of some one to call his Lady! There was, so the story goes, in a village near his own a very good-looking farm-girl with whom he had been at one time in love, though, so far as is known, she never knew it nor gave a thought to the matter. Her name was Aldonza Lorenzo, and upon her he thought fit to confer the title of Lady of his Thoughts; and after some search for a name which should not be out of harmony with her own, and should suggest and indicate that of a princess and great lady, he decided upon calling her Dulcinea del Toboso—she being of El Toboso—a name, to his mind, musical, uncommon, and significant, like all those he had already bestowed upon himself and the things belonging to him.

p007b.jpg (61K)

CHAPTER II.: WHICH TREATS OF THE FIRST SALLY THE INGENIOUS DON QUIXOTE MADE FROM HOME

p007c.jpg (97K)

These preliminaries settled, he did not care to put off any longer the execution of his design, urged on to it by the thought of all the world was losing by his delay, seeing what wrongs he intended to right, grievances to redress, injustices to repair, abuses to remove, and duties to discharge. So, without giving notice of his intention to anyone, and without anybody seeing him, one morning before the dawning of the day (which was one of the hottest of the month of July) he donned his suit of armour, mounted Rocinante with his patched-up helmet on, braced his buckler, took his lance, and by the back door of the yard sallied forth upon the plain in the highest contentment and satisfaction at seeing with what ease he had made a beginning with his grand purpose. But scarcely did he find himself upon the open plain, when a terrible thought struck him, one all but enough to make him abandon the enterprise at the very outset. It occurred to him that he had not been dubbed a knight, and that according to the law of chivalry he neither could nor ought to bear arms against any knight; and that even if he had been, still he ought, as a novice knight, to wear white armour, without a device upon the shield until by his prowess he had earned one. These reflections made him waver in his purpose, but his craze being stronger than any reasoning, he made up his mind to have himself dubbed a knight by the first one he came across, following the example of others in the same case, as he had read in the books that brought him to this pass. As for white armour, he resolved, on the first opportunity, to scour his until it was whiter than an ermine; and so comforting himself he pursued his way, taking that which his horse chose, for in this he believed lay the essence of adventures.

Thus setting out, our new-fledged adventurer paced along, talking to himself and saying, "Who knows but that in time to come, when the veracious history of my famous deeds is made known, the sage who writes it, when he has to set forth my first sally in the early morning, will do it after this fashion? 'Scarce had the rubicund Apollo spread o'er the face of the broad spacious earth the golden threads of his bright hair, scarce had the little birds of painted plumage attuned their notes to hail with dulcet and mellifluous harmony the coming of the rosy Dawn, that, deserting the soft couch of her jealous spouse, was appearing to mortals at the gates and balconies of the Manchegan horizon, when the renowned knight Don Quixote of La Mancha, quitting the lazy down, mounted his celebrated steed Rocinante and began to traverse the ancient and famous Campo de Montiel;'" which in fact he was actually traversing. "Happy the age, happy the time," he continued, "in which shall be made known my deeds of fame, worthy to be moulded in brass, carved in marble, limned in pictures, for a memorial for ever. And thou, O sage magician, whoever thou art, to whom it shall fall to be the chronicler of this wondrous history, forget not, I entreat thee, my good Rocinante, the constant companion of my ways and wanderings." Presently he broke out again, as if he were love-stricken in earnest, "O Princess Dulcinea, lady of this captive heart, a grievous wrong hast thou done me to drive me forth with scorn, and with inexorable obduracy banish me from the presence of thy beauty. O lady, deign to hold in remembrance this heart, thy vassal, that thus in anguish pines for love of thee."

So he went on stringing together these and other absurdities, all in the style of those his books had taught him, imitating their language as well as he could; and all the while he rode so slowly and the sun mounted so rapidly and with such fervour that it was enough to melt his brains if he had any. Nearly all day he travelled without anything remarkable happening to him, at which he was in despair, for he was anxious to encounter some one at once upon whom to try the might of his strong arm.

p008.jpg (289K)

Writers there are who say the first adventure he met with was that of Puerto Lapice; others say it was that of the windmills; but what I have ascertained on this point, and what I have found written in the annals of La Mancha, is that he was on the road all day, and towards nightfall his hack and he found themselves dead tired and hungry, when, looking all around to see if he could discover any castle or shepherd's shanty where he might refresh himself and relieve his sore wants, he perceived not far out of his road an inn, which was as welcome as a star guiding him to the portals, if not the palaces, of his redemption; and quickening his pace he reached it just as night was setting in. At the door were standing two young women, girls of the district as they call them, on their way to Seville with some carriers who had chanced to halt that night at the inn; and as, happen what might to our adventurer, everything he saw or imaged seemed to him to be and to happen after the fashion of what he read of, the moment he saw the inn he pictured it to himself as a castle with its four turrets and pinnacles of shining silver, not forgetting the drawbridge and moat and all the belongings usually ascribed to castles of the sort. To this inn, which to him seemed a castle, he advanced, and at a short distance from it he checked Rocinante, hoping that some dwarf would show himself upon the battlements, and by sound of trumpet give notice that a knight was approaching the castle. But seeing that they were slow about it, and that Rocinante was in a hurry to reach the stable, he made for the inn door, and perceived the two gay damsels who were standing there, and who seemed to him to be two fair maidens or lovely ladies taking their ease at the castle gate.

At this moment it so happened that a swineherd who was going through the stubbles collecting a drove of pigs (for, without any apology, that is what they are called) gave a blast of his horn to bring them together, and forthwith it seemed to Don Quixote to be what he was expecting, the signal of some dwarf announcing his arrival; and so with prodigious satisfaction he rode up to the inn and to the ladies, who, seeing a man of this sort approaching in full armour and with lance and buckler, were turning in dismay into the inn, when Don Quixote, guessing their fear by their flight, raising his pasteboard visor, disclosed his dry dusty visage, and with courteous bearing and gentle voice addressed them, "Your ladyships need not fly or fear any rudeness, for that it belongs not to the order of knighthood which I profess to offer to anyone, much less to highborn maidens as your appearance proclaims you to be." The girls were looking at him and straining their eyes to make out the features which the clumsy visor obscured, but when they heard themselves called maidens, a thing so much out of their line, they could not restrain their laughter, which made Don Quixote wax indignant, and say, "Modesty becomes the fair, and moreover laughter that has little cause is great silliness; this, however, I say not to pain or anger you, for my desire is none other than to serve you."

The incomprehensible language and the unpromising looks of our cavalier only increased the ladies' laughter, and that increased his irritation, and matters might have gone farther if at that moment the landlord had not come out, who, being a very fat man, was a very peaceful one. He, seeing this grotesque figure clad in armour that did not match any more than his saddle, bridle, lance, buckler, or corselet, was not at all indisposed to join the damsels in their manifestations of amusement; but, in truth, standing in awe of such a complicated armament, he thought it best to speak him fairly, so he said, "Senor Caballero, if your worship wants lodging, bating the bed (for there is not one in the inn) there is plenty of everything else here." Don Quixote, observing the respectful bearing of the Alcaide of the fortress (for so innkeeper and inn seemed in his eyes), made answer, "Sir Castellan, for me anything will suffice, for

My only rest the fray.""My armour is my only wear,

The host fancied he called him Castellan because he took him for a "worthy of Castile," though he was in fact an Andalusian, and one from the strand of San Lucar, as crafty a thief as Cacus and as full of tricks as a student or a page. "In that case," said he,

Your sleep to watch alway;""Your bed is on the flinty rock,

and if so, you may dismount and safely reckon upon any quantity of sleeplessness under this roof for a twelvemonth, not to say for a single night." So saying, he advanced to hold the stirrup for Don Quixote, who got down with great difficulty and exertion (for he had not broken his fast all day), and then charged the host to take great care of his horse, as he was the best bit of flesh that ever ate bread in this world. The landlord eyed him over but did not find him as good as Don Quixote said, nor even half as good; and putting him up in the stable, he returned to see what might be wanted by his guest, whom the damsels, who had by this time made their peace with him, were now relieving of his armour. They had taken off his breastplate and backpiece, but they neither knew nor saw how to open his gorget or remove his make-shift helmet, for he had fastened it with green ribbons, which, as there was no untying the knots, required to be cut. This, however, he would not by any means consent to, so he remained all the evening with his helmet on, the drollest and oddest figure that can be imagined; and while they were removing his armour, taking the baggages who were about it for ladies of high degree belonging to the castle, he said to them with great sprightliness:

—or Rocinante, for that, ladies mine, is my horse's name, and Don Quixote of La Mancha is my own; for though I had no intention of declaring myself until my achievements in your service and honour had made me known, the necessity of adapting that old ballad of Lancelot to the present occasion has given you the knowledge of my name altogether prematurely. A time, however, will come for your ladyships to command and me to obey, and then the might of my arm will show my desire to serve you."

The girls, who were not used to hearing rhetoric of this sort, had nothing to say in reply; they only asked him if he wanted anything to eat. "I would gladly eat a bit of something," said Don Quixote, "for I feel it would come very seasonably." The day happened to be a Friday, and in the whole inn there was nothing but some pieces of the fish they call in Castile "abadejo," in Andalusia "bacallao," and in some places "curadillo," and in others "troutlet;" so they asked him if he thought he could eat troutlet, for there was no other fish to give him. "If there be troutlets enough," said Don Quixote, "they will be the same thing as a trout; for it is all one to me whether I am given eight reals in small change or a piece of eight; moreover, it may be that these troutlets are like veal, which is better than beef, or kid, which is better than goat. But whatever it be let it come quickly, for the burden and pressure of arms cannot be borne without support to the inside." They laid a table for him at the door of the inn for the sake of the air, and the host brought him a portion of ill-soaked and worse cooked stockfish, and a piece of bread as black and mouldy as his own armour; but a laughable sight it was to see him eating, for having his helmet on and the beaver up, he could not with his own hands put anything into his mouth unless some one else placed it there, and this service one of the ladies rendered him. But to give him anything to drink was impossible, or would have been so had not the landlord bored a reed, and putting one end in his mouth poured the wine into him through the other; all which he bore with patience rather than sever the ribbons of his helmet.

While this was going on there came up to the inn a sowgelder, who, as he approached, sounded his reed pipe four or five times, and thereby completely convinced Don Quixote that he was in some famous castle, and that they were regaling him with music, and that the stockfish was trout, the bread the whitest, the wenches ladies, and the landlord the castellan of the castle; and consequently he held that his enterprise and sally had been to some purpose. But still it distressed him to think he had not been dubbed a knight, for it was plain to him he could not lawfully engage in any adventure without receiving the order of knighthood.

e02.jpg (39K)

CHAPTER III.: WHEREIN IS RELATED THE DROLL WAY IN WHICH DON QUIXOTE HAD HIMSELF DUBBED A KNIGHT

p009.jpg (164K)

Harassed by this reflection, he made haste with his scanty pothouse supper, and having finished it called the landlord, and shutting himself into the stable with him, fell on his knees before him, saying, "From this spot I rise not, valiant knight, until your courtesy grants me the boon I seek, one that will redound to your praise and the benefit of the human race." The landlord, seeing his guest at his feet and hearing a speech of this kind, stood staring at him in bewilderment, not knowing what to do or say, and entreating him to rise, but all to no purpose until he had agreed to grant the boon demanded of him. "I looked for no less, my lord, from your High Magnificence," replied Don Quixote, "and I have to tell you that the boon I have asked and your liberality has granted is that you shall dub me knight to-morrow morning, and that to-night I shall watch my arms in the chapel of this your castle; thus tomorrow, as I have said, will be accomplished what I so much desire, enabling me lawfully to roam through all the four quarters of the world seeking adventures on behalf of those in distress, as is the duty of chivalry and of knights-errant like myself, whose ambition is directed to such deeds."

The landlord, who, as has been mentioned, was something of a wag, and had already some suspicion of his guest's want of wits, was quite convinced of it on hearing talk of this kind from him, and to make sport for the night he determined to fall in with his humour. So he told him he was quite right in pursuing the object he had in view, and that such a motive was natural and becoming in cavaliers as distinguished as he seemed and his gallant bearing showed him to be; and that he himself in his younger days had followed the same honourable calling, roaming in quest of adventures in various parts of the world, among others the Curing-grounds of Malaga, the Isles of Riaran, the Precinct of Seville, the Little Market of Segovia, the Olivera of Valencia, the Rondilla of Granada, the Strand of San Lucar, the Colt of Cordova, the Taverns of Toledo, and divers other quarters, where he had proved the nimbleness of his feet and the lightness of his fingers, doing many wrongs, cheating many widows, ruining maids and swindling minors, and, in short, bringing himself under the notice of almost every tribunal and court of justice in Spain; until at last he had retired to this castle of his, where he was living upon his property and upon that of others; and where he received all knights-errant of whatever rank or condition they might be, all for the great love he bore them and that they might share their substance with him in return for his benevolence. He told him, moreover, that in this castle of his there was no chapel in which he could watch his armour, as it had been pulled down in order to be rebuilt, but that in a case of necessity it might, he knew, be watched anywhere, and he might watch it that night in a courtyard of the castle, and in the morning, God willing, the requisite ceremonies might be performed so as to have him dubbed a knight, and so thoroughly dubbed that nobody could be more so. He asked if he had any money with him, to which Don Quixote replied that he had not a farthing, as in the histories of knights-errant he had never read of any of them carrying any. On this point the landlord told him he was mistaken; for, though not recorded in the histories, because in the author's opinion there was no need to mention anything so obvious and necessary as money and clean shirts, it was not to be supposed therefore that they did not carry them, and he might regard it as certain and established that all knights-errant (about whom there were so many full and unimpeachable books) carried well-furnished purses in case of emergency, and likewise carried shirts and a little box of ointment to cure the wounds they received. For in those plains and deserts where they engaged in combat and came out wounded, it was not always that there was some one to cure them, unless indeed they had for a friend some sage magician to succour them at once by fetching through the air upon a cloud some damsel or dwarf with a vial of water of such virtue that by tasting one drop of it they were cured of their hurts and wounds in an instant and left as sound as if they had not received any damage whatever. But in case this should not occur, the knights of old took care to see that their squires were provided with money and other requisites, such as lint and ointments for healing purposes; and when it happened that knights had no squires (which was rarely and seldom the case) they themselves carried everything in cunning saddle-bags that were hardly seen on the horse's croup, as if it were something else of more importance, because, unless for some such reason, carrying saddle-bags was not very favourably regarded among knights-errant. He therefore advised him (and, as his godson so soon to be, he might even command him) never from that time forth to travel without money and the usual requirements, and he would find the advantage of them when he least expected it.

Don Quixote promised to follow his advice scrupulously, and it was arranged forthwith that he should watch his armour in a large yard at one side of the inn; so, collecting it all together, Don Quixote placed it on a trough that stood by the side of a well, and bracing his buckler on his arm he grasped his lance and began with a stately air to march up and down in front of the trough, and as he began his march night began to fall.

The landlord told all the people who were in the inn about the craze of his guest, the watching of the armour, and the dubbing ceremony he contemplated. Full of wonder at so strange a form of madness, they flocked to see it from a distance, and observed with what composure he sometimes paced up and down, or sometimes, leaning on his lance, gazed on his armour without taking his eyes off it for ever so long; and as the night closed in with a light from the moon so brilliant that it might vie with his that lent it, everything the novice knight did was plainly seen by all.

Meanwhile one of the carriers who were in the inn thought fit to water his team, and it was necessary to remove Don Quixote's armour as it lay on the trough; but he seeing the other approach hailed him in a loud voice, "O thou, whoever thou art, rash knight that comest to lay hands on the armour of the most valorous errant that ever girt on sword, have a care what thou dost; touch it not unless thou wouldst lay down thy life as the penalty of thy rashness." The carrier gave no heed to these words (and he would have done better to heed them if he had been heedful of his health), but seizing it by the straps flung the armour some distance from him. Seeing this, Don Quixote raised his eyes to heaven, and fixing his thoughts, apparently, upon his lady Dulcinea, exclaimed, "Aid me, lady mine, in this the first encounter that presents itself to this breast which thou holdest in subjection; let not thy favour and protection fail me in this first jeopardy;" and, with these words and others to the same purpose, dropping his buckler he lifted his lance with both hands and with it smote such a blow on the carrier's head that he stretched him on the ground, so stunned that had he followed it up with a second there would have been no need of a surgeon to cure him. This done, he picked up his armour and returned to his beat with the same serenity as before.

p010.jpg (261K)

Shortly after this, another, not knowing what had happened (for the carrier still lay senseless), came with the same object of giving water to his mules, and was proceeding to remove the armour in order to clear the trough, when Don Quixote, without uttering a word or imploring aid from anyone, once more dropped his buckler and once more lifted his lance, and without actually breaking the second carrier's head into pieces, made more than three of it, for he laid it open in four. At the noise all the people of the inn ran to the spot, and among them the landlord. Seeing this, Don Quixote braced his buckler on his arm, and with his hand on his sword exclaimed, "O Lady of Beauty, strength and support of my faint heart, it is time for thee to turn the eyes of thy greatness on this thy captive knight on the brink of so mighty an adventure." By this he felt himself so inspired that he would not have flinched if all the carriers in the world had assailed him. The comrades of the wounded perceiving the plight they were in began from a distance to shower stones on Don Quixote, who screened himself as best he could with his buckler, not daring to quit the trough and leave his armour unprotected. The landlord shouted to them to leave him alone, for he had already told them that he was mad, and as a madman he would not be accountable even if he killed them all. Still louder shouted Don Quixote, calling them knaves and traitors, and the lord of the castle, who allowed knights-errant to be treated in this fashion, a villain and a low-born knight whom, had he received the order of knighthood, he would call to account for his treachery. "But of you," he cried, "base and vile rabble, I make no account; fling, strike, come on, do all ye can against me, ye shall see what the reward of your folly and insolence will be." This he uttered with so much spirit and boldness that he filled his assailants with a terrible fear, and as much for this reason as at the persuasion of the landlord they left off stoning him, and he allowed them to carry off the wounded, and with the same calmness and composure as before resumed the watch over his armour.

But these freaks of his guest were not much to the liking of the landlord, so he determined to cut matters short and confer upon him at once the unlucky order of knighthood before any further misadventure could occur; so, going up to him, he apologised for the rudeness which, without his knowledge, had been offered to him by these low people, who, however, had been well punished for their audacity. As he had already told him, he said, there was no chapel in the castle, nor was it needed for what remained to be done, for, as he understood the ceremonial of the order, the whole point of being dubbed a knight lay in the accolade and in the slap on the shoulder, and that could be administered in the middle of a field; and that he had now done all that was needful as to watching the armour, for all requirements were satisfied by a watch of two hours only, while he had been more than four about it. Don Quixote believed it all, and told him he stood there ready to obey him, and to make an end of it with as much despatch as possible; for, if he were again attacked, and felt himself to be dubbed knight, he would not, he thought, leave a soul alive in the castle, except such as out of respect he might spare at his bidding.

Thus warned and menaced, the castellan forthwith brought out a book in which he used to enter the straw and barley he served out to the carriers, and, with a lad carrying a candle-end, and the two damsels already mentioned, he returned to where Don Quixote stood, and bade him kneel down. Then, reading from his account-book as if he were repeating some devout prayer, in the middle of his delivery he raised his hand and gave him a sturdy blow on the neck, and then, with his own sword, a smart slap on the shoulder, all the while muttering between his teeth as if he was saying his prayers. Having done this, he directed one of the ladies to gird on his sword, which she did with great self-possession and gravity, and not a little was required to prevent a burst of laughter at each stage of the ceremony; but what they had already seen of the novice knight's prowess kept their laughter within bounds. On girding him with the sword the worthy lady said to him, "May God make your worship a very fortunate knight, and grant you success in battle." Don Quixote asked her name in order that he might from that time forward know to whom he was beholden for the favour he had received, as he meant to confer upon her some portion of the honour he acquired by the might of his arm. She answered with great humility that she was called La Tolosa, and that she was the daughter of a cobbler of Toledo who lived in the stalls of Sanchobienaya, and that wherever she might be she would serve and esteem him as her lord. Don Quixote said in reply that she would do him a favour if thenceforward she assumed the "Don" and called herself Dona Tolosa. She promised she would, and then the other buckled on his spur, and with her followed almost the same conversation as with the lady of the sword. He asked her name, and she said it was La Molinera, and that she was the daughter of a respectable miller of Antequera; and of her likewise Don Quixote requested that she would adopt the "Don" and call herself Dona Molinera, making offers to her further services and favours.

Having thus, with hot haste and speed, brought to a conclusion these never-till-now-seen ceremonies, Don Quixote was on thorns until he saw himself on horseback sallying forth in quest of adventures; and saddling Rocinante at once he mounted, and embracing his host, as he returned thanks for his kindness in knighting him, he addressed him in language so extraordinary that it is impossible to convey an idea of it or report it. The landlord, to get him out of the inn, replied with no less rhetoric though with shorter words, and without calling upon him to pay the reckoning let him go with a Godspeed.

p017.jpg (54K)

Printed in Great Britain
by Amazon